OSCAR THE GROUCH!

Zoe

Cookie Monster

Count Von Count

THIS BOOK BELONGS TO:

BERT

Snuffy

Prairie Dawn

D1174523

Designed by Bendon Publishing International, Inc.

ISBN-13: 978-1-4351-4258-9

Manufactured in China
Lot #:
2 4 6 8 10 9 7 5 3 1
06/12

123 SESAME STREET®

GROVER

Takes Care of BABY

by Emily Thompson

illustrated by
Tom Cooke

Sandy Creek
NEW YORK

One day Grover dropped his ball, and it rolled under a baby carriage.

"Oh, hello, Marsha!" said Grover. "Who is this?"

"This is my baby brother," said Marsha. "I'm taking care of him. I play with him, take him for walks, help him, give him his baths, and put him to bed."

"I have a baby cousin, named Emily. I, lovable, old Grover, would take good care of baby Emily," said Grover. Grover waved good-bye to Marsha and Max.

I would let her play with my toys.

I would show Emily how to climb mountains...

go through tunnels...

and leap tall buildings in a single bound!

If Baby Emily came for a visit, she could take a nap in my zoo.

I would help her get dressed.

I would introduce Emily to all of my friends at
play group. Oh, I would be so proud!

But what if she tore my picture? Oh, I would be so embarrassed!

Mrs. Brown would say, "Never mind, Grover, we can fix it."

After play group, we could go shopping...

and for a walk.

We could do our exercises together. One and two and—pant, pant!—three. Now touch those toes!

We could play peekaboo...

and eensy-weensy spider.

At dinnertime, I would help my mommy feed Emily.
I would tie on her bib, and wipe up her dribbles.

"Emily, sweetie, you need a bath. You are a mess!"

At bath time, I would be ready.

I would pour in the bubbles...

and test the temperature.

Then I would duck.

At bedtime, I would help Emily listen to a story.

Then I would sing her a lullaby, kiss her nose,
and turn on the night-light. I would even let her
borrow my teddy monster to cuddle.

"Good night, Baby Emily."

"I, Grover, would be a big help," he said proudly.

"Grover, you are very good at taking care of
baby monster!" said his mommy.